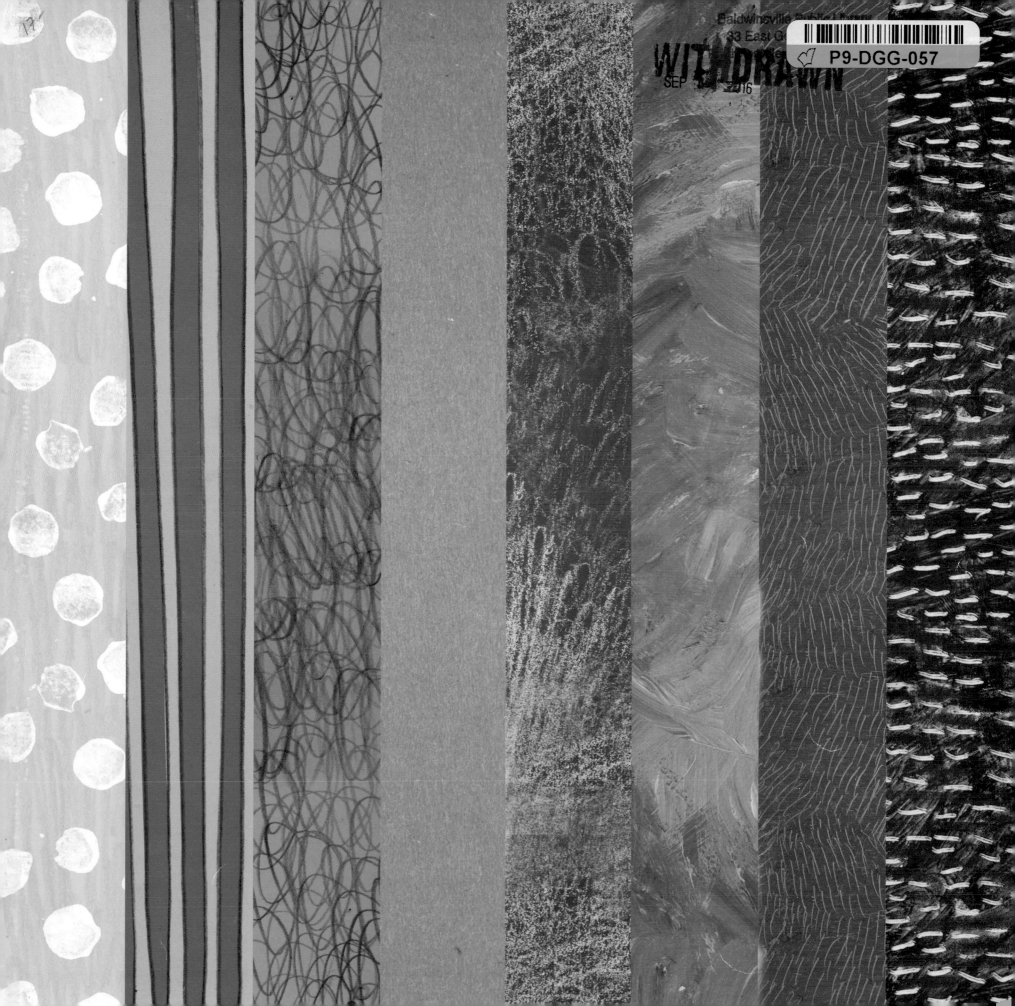

For my dear little Monster Sidney, who prefers ALL to be WIDE-AWAKE

First U.S. edition 2016

SEP 1 4 2016

Library of Congress Catalog Card Number 2015937225

ISBN 978-0-7636-8660-4

GBL 21 20 19 18 17 16

10 9 8 7 6 5 4 3 2 1

Printed in Shenzhen, Guangdong, China

This book was typeset in Noasarck.
The illustrations were created digitally.

Nosy Crow
an imprint of
Candlewick Press
99 Dover Street
Somerville, Massachusetts 02144

www.nosycrow.com
www.candlewick.com

The BIG MONSTER SnoreYBOOK

LEIGH HODGKINSON

nosy crow

An imprint of Candlewick Press

Oh, dear. What bad timing.

There doesn't seem to be anything going on in this book right now.

You see, EVERYBODY'S asleep.

If you don't believe me, you can take a peek for yourself.

But—just so you know—they are very snorey!

First is **norris.**

He has a monster cold. While he sleeps,
his tiny toothypegs chitter and chatter
and his knobbly knees knock.

They never stop talking.
They even jibber-jabber and bibble-babble in their sleep!

Next is **TONY.**

Tony's toes tippy-tap while he dreams.

Those terribly tatty toenails make a lot of noise!

GROWL

GRUMBLY

RUMBLY

Last of all is **BRIAN.**

Brian is always hungry!
His big belly gurgles and growls all night long.

So, that's it—ALL the monsters in this book.

All asleep.

Oh, no! The monsters have all woken up!
And after a snooze, monsters are always VERY hungry.

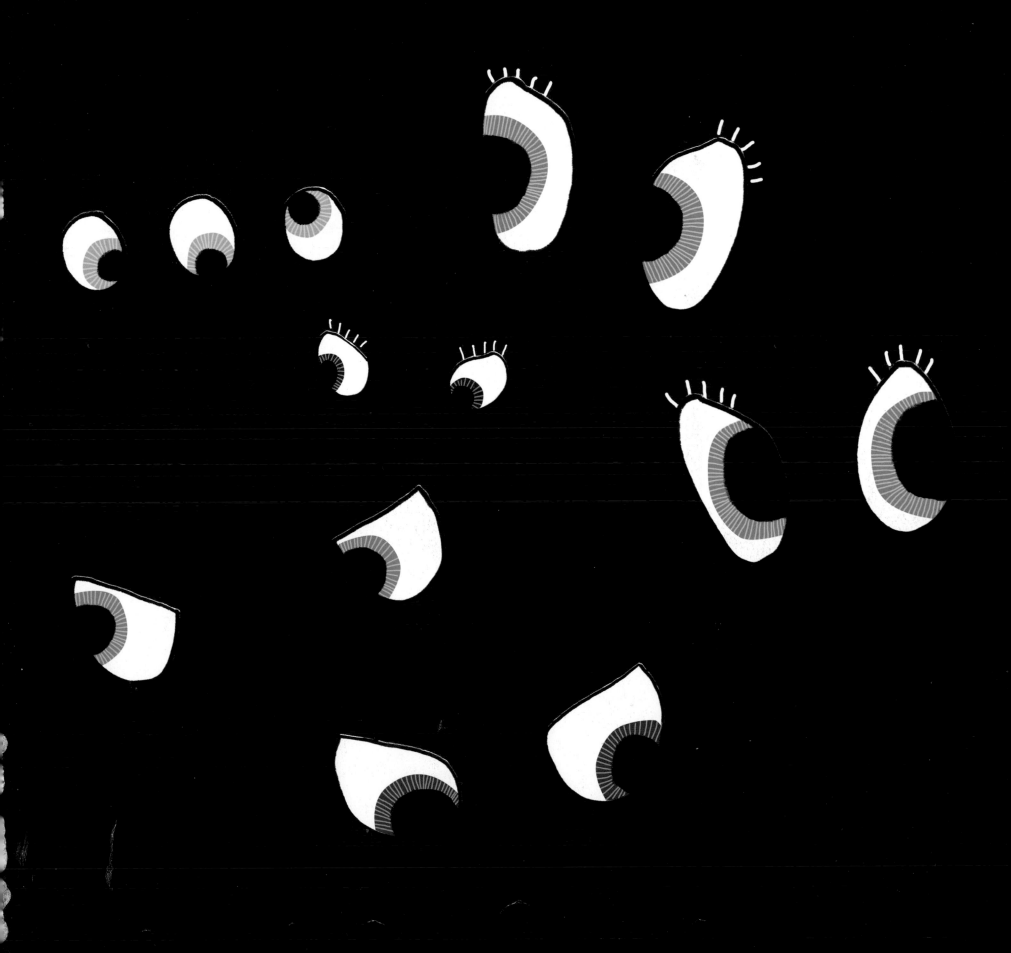

Now the monsters will look for some little monsters to eat.

Good thing there aren't any of those around!

chitter

JIBBER JABBER

TIPPY

THUD

THUMP THUNK

RUMBLY

GRUMBLY

Chatter

BIBBLE BABBLE

TAP TAP

SCRITCH SCRATCH SCRITCH

GROWL

Oh, my! It sounds like an even BIGGER and even HUNGRIER monster just woke up!

And it's headed this way!

Well, that seems to have scared everybody away,

so now it's nice and quiet.

Good night!

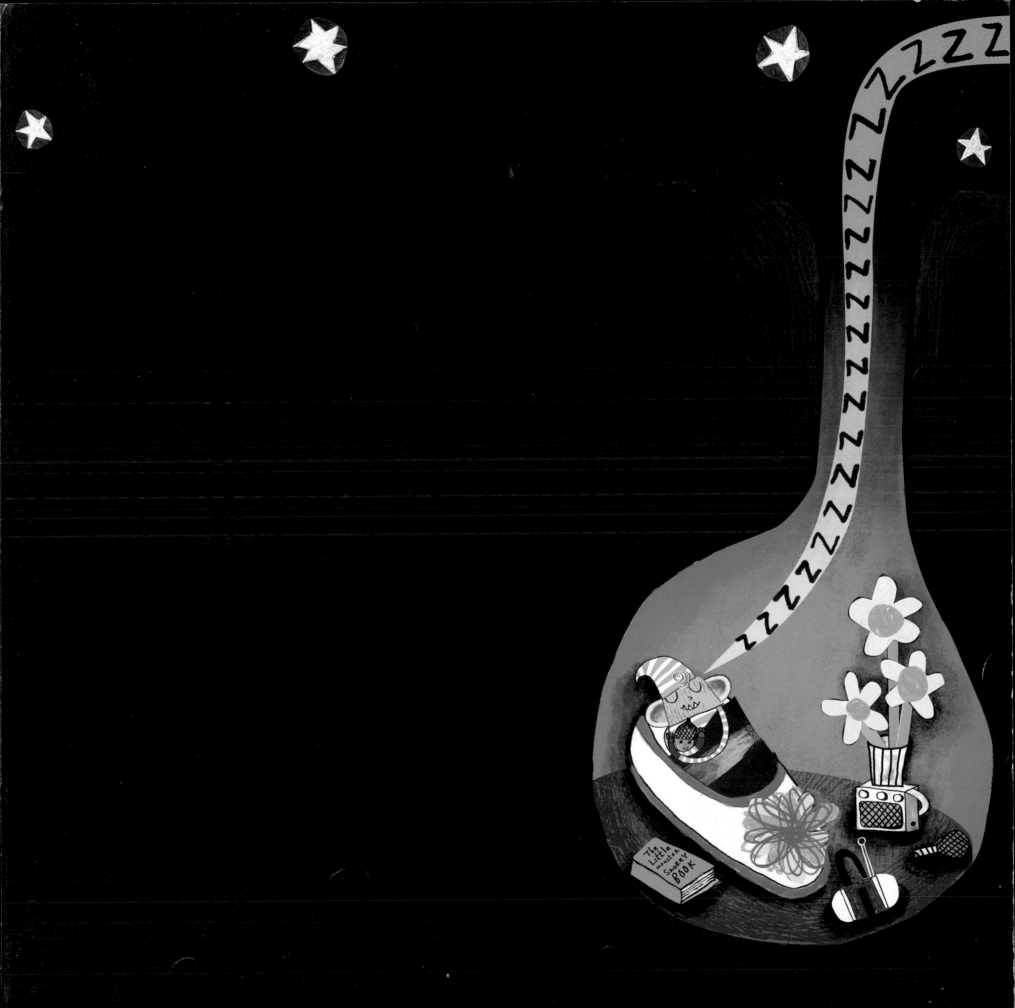